AF578058

Forbidden Freedom

Michael Gordon

Published by MG Books, 2024.

This is a work of fiction. Similarities to real people, places, or events are entirely coincidental.

FORBIDDEN FREEDOM

First edition. November 23, 2024.

Copyright © 2024 Michael Gordon.

ISBN: 979-8230517603

Written by Michael Gordon.

Table of Contents

Chapter 1

The city buzzed with revolutionary fervor as the warm summer sun shone down on its bustling streets. Amidst the chaos of the ongoing war, a young woman with fiery determination in her eyes marched towards the town center, her red hair flowing gracefully in the gentle breeze. Martha Wright, a vision of strength and beauty, was on a mission—a mission to fight for the freedom she believed every human deserved.

As Martha navigated the crowded lanes, her pale skin stood out among the sea of tanned faces. Her green eyes scanned the surroundings, taking in the lively atmosphere. The air was thick with the scent of freshly baked bread from nearby bakeries, intermingled with the less pleasant odors of horse manure and unwashed bodies. Philadelphia, like most cities of that era, was a stark contrast of grandeur and grime.

Martha's destination was the town square, where a protest was about to take place. The fight for the abolition of slavery had been gaining momentum, and Martha, along with her parents, was at the forefront of this movement. The Wright family owned a local newspaper, which they used as a platform to voice their strong anti-slavery sentiments. Their words had stirred the hearts of many, and today, Martha intended to let her actions speak louder than any printed page.

Reaching the square, Martha was greeted by a sea of people, their voices echoing off the brick buildings that lined the dirt streets. The crowd was a diverse mix of abolitionists, freed slaves, and curious onlookers. Martha spotted a group of her friends, all young women who shared her passion for equality. They waved enthusiastically, their eyes filled with determination and a hint of fear, for they knew the potential consequences of their actions.

"Martha!" exclaimed Sarah, her closest friend, as she pushed through the crowd to reach her. "Are you ready for this? It might get ugly."

Martha smiled, her confidence unwavering. "I'm ready. We've been preparing for this moment, and I won't let fear silence me. Our voices must be heard, no matter the cost."

As the protest began, Martha's heart pounded in her chest. She stood tall, her eyes fixed on the city hall building, where the town's officials and slave owners had gathered. The crowd chanted in unison, their voices rising in a powerful wave. "Freedom for all! End slavery now!"

The atmosphere was tense, with a palpable undercurrent of anger and frustration. The protesters held up signs and banners, each one a declaration of their beliefs. Martha's sign read, "Equality is the birthright of every human," and she held it high, her voice joining the chorus of dissent.

Suddenly, a commotion erupted at the edge of the square. A group of angry men, their faces twisted with rage, pushed through the crowd, brandishing sticks and makeshift weapons. They were the supporters of the slave owners, determined to silence the protesters by any means necessary.

The peaceful protest quickly descended into chaos. The mob attacked the demonstrators, and the square became a battleground. Martha found herself in the midst of the fray, her sign dropping to the ground as she struggled to keep her balance. A burly man with a scarred face lunged at her, his eyes wild with fury.

Just as the man's meaty fist was about to connect with Martha's face, a dark figure emerged from the chaos. With lightning-fast reflexes, he intercepted the blow, his muscular arm deflecting the attack. The man was sent reeling, his momentum carrying him to the ground.

Martha, startled and grateful, turned to thank her savior. Her eyes met those of a tall, African man with a powerful build. His dark skin was marred by multiple scars on his back, a testament to the horrors he had endured as a slave. Despite his imposing stature, his eyes held a softness that contradicted his rugged appearance.

"Are you alright, miss?" he asked, his voice gentle and deep.

Martha, momentarily speechless, nodded, her heart still racing. "Yes, thank you. You saved me."

The man offered her a small smile, his teeth flashing white against his dark skin. "It was my pleasure. I couldn't stand by and watch you get hurt."

As they spoke, the riot continued to rage around them. The man, who introduced himself as Thomas Freeman, moved with purpose, guiding Martha away from the worst of the violence. His strength and agility were evident as he cleared a path through the chaos, his large hands gently but firmly guiding Martha to safety.

"This way, miss," he said, his voice calm amidst the chaos. "We need to get you out of here."

Martha, caught up in the moment, allowed herself to be led by this mysterious man. As they reached the outskirts of the square, the sound of the riot began to fade. Thomas paused, his breath coming in short gasps, his powerful chest rising and falling with each breath. Martha realized with a start that he had been injured in the scuffle, his shirt torn, revealing the scars that marked his back.

"You're hurt," she said, her voice filled with concern. "Let me help you."

Thomas shook his head, his eyes never leaving hers. "I'm fine, really. Just a few scratches. But you, you could have been seriously injured back there. It's not safe for a woman like you to be in the midst of such violence."

Martha's eyes flashed with determination. "I can take care of myself, and I won't be silenced by fear. But I'm grateful for your help. You fought for me when others might have turned away."

Thomas smiled, a warm expression that transformed his rugged features. "I couldn't just stand by. I saw the way you stood up for what you believed in, and it reminded me of someone I once knew. A woman who fought for what was right, no matter the cost."

Intrigued, Martha found herself drawn to this man, his gentle strength and quiet courage captivating her. "Who was she?" she asked, her voice soft.

Thomas paused, his eyes distant as he recalled a memory. "My mother. She was a strong woman, and she raised me to stand up for what I believed in, even when it seemed impossible. She taught me that love and respect are the foundations of a just world."

Martha's heart skipped a beat. Here was a man who understood the true meaning of love and equality, a man who had endured unimaginable hardships yet remained kind and compassionate. She found herself wanting to know more about him, to understand the man behind the scars.

"Thomas, I—" she began, but her words were cut short as the sound of approaching hooves filled the air. A group of men on horseback, rode towards them.

"Run!" Thomas shouted, his voice filled with urgency.

Without hesitation, Martha and Thomas sprinted down a narrow alley, their footsteps echoing off the brick walls. The riders pursued them, their horses' hooves clattering on the cobblestones. Thomas, with his powerful strides, kept Martha close, his hand protectively on her back.

They weaved through the maze of back alleys, the riders hot on their trail. Just as they emerged onto a wider street, Thomas pushed Martha behind a stack of crates, shielding her with his body. The riders thundered past, their eyes scanning the area.

As the coast cleared, Thomas helped Martha to her feet. "We need to get you to safety," he said, his voice filled with concern. "These men won't give up easily."

Martha, her heart still pounding, looked up at Thomas, her green eyes sparkling with gratitude. "Thank you, again. I don't know what I would have done without you."

Thomas smiled, his eyes holding hers. "I won't leave your side until I know you're safe. And perhaps, if you'll allow it, I'd like to get to know you better. I sense there's more to you than meets the eye, Martha Wright."

Martha felt her cheeks warm at his words. This man, a former slave, was offering to court her, a white woman of privilege. She knew the implications of such an arrangement, the potential backlash from society, but in that moment, none of it mattered. She saw the man Thomas was—a man of strength, compassion, and unwavering principles.

"I would like that, Thomas Freeman," she replied, her voice steady. "I believe love isn't bound by the color of one's skin. And I see the man you are, not the scars that mark your past."

Thomas's smile widened, his eyes softening as he took her hand in his. "Then let's leave this place and find a quiet spot where we can talk, away from prying eyes and angry mobs."

Hand in hand, they made their way through the city, the chaos of the riot fading into the background. They found a secluded spot by the river, where the water gently lapped at the shore, providing a soothing backdrop to their conversation.

As they sat, Thomas told Martha of his life as a slave, the hardships he had endured, and the strength he had found within himself to survive. He spoke of his dreams for a future where all men and women, regardless of their skin color, could live in harmony and love freely. Martha listened, captivated by his words and the passion in his voice.

"You have a beautiful soul, Thomas," she said, reaching out to touch his hand. "And I believe your dreams can become a reality. We must keep fighting, and together, we can make a difference."

Thomas leaned in, his eyes searching hers. "And I believe that you, Martha Wright, are the kind of woman who can change the world. Your passion and strength are infectious, and I want to be by your side as we fight for what's right."

Martha felt her heart flutter, her cheeks flushing at his words. This man, who had saved her from harm and shared his deepest thoughts, was offering her more than just his protection. He was offering his heart, and she found herself wanting to accept it.

As the sun began to set, casting a golden glow over the river, Martha and Thomas sat in silence, their hands intertwined. The attraction between them was undeniable, a connection forged in the heat of battle and strengthened by their shared ideals.

"Thomas," Martha began, her voice soft and hesitant. "I want to see you again. I want to know more about you, and I want to explore this... this connection we have."

Thomas's eyes lit up, and he brought her hand to his lips, placing a gentle kiss on her knuckles. "I would like that, Martha. More than you know. But I must warn you, courting a black man in this time is not without its dangers. Society will not look kindly upon us."

Martha's determination shone in her eyes. "I don't care what society thinks, Thomas. I've always been an outspoken woman, and I won't let others dictate my heart. If you're willing to take the risk, so am I."

Thomas smiled, his heart overflowing with joy and hope. "Then let's make a pact, you and I. We'll face the world together, hand in hand, and let our love be a beacon of hope in these dark times. We'll show them that love transcends color and class."

Chapter 2

The city of Philadelphia buzzed with a mix of excitement and tension as the year 1779 unfolded. The air was thick with the scent of change, and the streets echoed with the voices of revolution. Among the bustling crowds, Martha Wright and Thomas Freeman found themselves drawn together by a force stronger than the political upheaval around them. Their secret courtship blossomed in the shadows of a society that sought to keep them apart.

In the weeks following their daring escape from the riot, Martha and Thomas met frequently under the guise of afternoon rides and leisurely picnics. They would ride their horses through the countryside, where the air was cleaner and the atmosphere more serene. Philadelphia's bustling streets and the constant threat of riots were left behind, allowing them to focus on each other. During these rides, they would stop by a secluded clearing near a babbling brook, where they laid out a blanket and shared a simple meal.

As they sat side by side, Martha's fiery red hair, a striking contrast to her pale skin, danced in the gentle breeze. Her green eyes sparkled with determination as she discussed her vision for a better world. Thomas, his dark skin glistening with a thin sheen of sweat from the ride, listened intently, his eyes never leaving her face. He was captivated by her passion and her unwavering commitment to freedom and equality. They talked about the state of the revolution, sharing their hopes and fears for the future. Martha's words flowed with an eloquence that matched her beauty, and Thomas found himself hanging on her every word.

"I believe in a world where all men and women are truly free, Thomas," Martha said, her voice carrying a hint of defiance. "A world where the

color of one's skin does not determine their worth. Where people like you, with strength and dignity, are not treated as property but as equals."
Thomas reached out and took her hand, his rough fingers entwining with hers. "I know, Martha. I've seen the power of your words in the pages of your parents' newspaper. You speak for those who cannot, and I admire your courage."

Martha smiled, her lips curving upwards, revealing a hint of mischief. "Then, my dear Thomas, let us continue to speak and fight for what is right. Together, we can make a difference."

Their picnics were not merely a time for discussion, but also a chance for them to share stolen moments of intimacy. As they finished their meal, Thomas would produce a bottle of wine, which they would drink from wooden cups, savoring the taste of freedom. They would lean into each other, their bodies touching, sharing the warmth that seemed to radiate from within. Martha's hand would often find its way to Thomas's face, tracing the lines of his scars, a reminder of the hardships he had endured. He would close his eyes, relishing the gentle touch, a stark contrast to the pain he had experienced in the past.

On one such afternoon, as the sun began its descent, casting a golden glow over the landscape, Martha and Thomas decided to return to the city. They mounted their horses and rode back towards Philadelphia, their hearts lighter than they had been in a long time. The horses' hooves beat a steady rhythm on the dirt roads, and the wind whispered through the trees, providing a soothing backdrop to their conversation.

"I want to take you somewhere special, Martha," Thomas said, his voice carrying a hint of nervousness. "A place that holds great significance for me."

Intrigued, Martha urged her horse closer to his. "I'd love to see it, Thomas. Is it far from here?"

"Not far at all. It's a place where I found refuge when I first arrived in Philadelphia. A place that gave me hope and a sense of belonging."

As they approached the city, Thomas guided them through the maze of dirt streets, past the bustling marketplaces and rowdy taverns. They eventually arrived at a modest brick building, nestled between a tailor's shop and a cobbler's. The sign above the door read 'The Freedom Center.'

"This is it," Thomas said, a sense of pride evident in his voice. "A place where freed slaves and abolitionists gather. It's a haven for those seeking a better life."

Martha's eyes widened as she took in the building. "I've heard of this place, Thomas. It's a beacon of hope for so many. To think we're standing right outside it..."

Thomas dismounted and offered his hand to help Martha down from her horse. As they stood side by side, he said, "I want you to meet some of the people who have become like family to me. They will understand our love, Martha, and support us."

Martha's heart raced as she followed Thomas inside. The Freedom Center was a warm and welcoming space, filled with laughter and the scent of fresh-baked bread. They were greeted by a group of men and women of various ages and backgrounds, all with stories of their own.

"Friends, I'd like you to meet Martha Wright," Thomas announced, his voice filled with pride. "A woman of extraordinary courage and compassion."

The group welcomed Martha with open arms, and she was soon engaged in lively conversations, sharing her experiences and learning about their struggles and triumphs. Thomas, meanwhile, stood by her side, a silent sentinel, his eyes never leaving her.

As the evening wore on, the group shared a simple meal, and the atmosphere became more intimate. Martha and Thomas found themselves sitting close together, their shoulders brushing as they listened to a man with a deep, melodic voice recount his journey to freedom.

"We must keep fighting, my friends," the man said, his eyes glistening with unshed tears. "For those still in chains and for those who have yet to break free."

His words resonated with Martha and Thomas, and they exchanged a knowing glance. In that moment, they both understood the power of their love and its potential to inspire change.

After the gathering, as they walked back to their horses, Martha took Thomas's hand, her fingers intertwining with his. "Thomas, I want you to know that I'm ready to stand by your side, publicly, if that's what you wish. I want to be a part of this movement, not just as an observer but as your partner."

Thomas stopped walking and turned to face her, his dark eyes shining with emotion. "Martha, my love, I've been waiting for you to say those words. I want the world to know that we stand together, that our love is a symbol of the freedom we fight for."

Martha smiled, her heart overflowing with joy. "Then let's make it official, Thomas. Let's get married, and let our union be a testament to the power of love and equality."

Thomas's face lit up with a broad smile, and he pulled her into a tight embrace. "Yes, Martha. Let's do it. Let's show the world that love knows no bounds and that freedom is a right for all."

In the days that followed, Martha and Thomas made preparations for their wedding. They met with a local pastor who understood and supported their cause. The pastor agreed to perform the ceremony in secret, away from prying eyes and the threat of backlash. The couple chose a secluded spot by the river, where the water's gentle flow mirrored the peacefulness they sought.

On the day of their wedding, the sun shone brightly, as if in celebration of their love. Martha, dressed in a simple yet elegant gown, her red hair cascading down her back, waited with anticipation. Thomas, handsome in a tailored suit, approached her, his eyes filled with love and admiration.

The pastor began the ceremony, his words echoing off the river's surface. He spoke of love, equality, and the power of unity. Martha and Thomas exchanged vows, their voices trembling with emotion.

"I, Martha, take you, Thomas, to be my husband, my partner in life, and my ally in the fight for freedom. I promise to love and support you, to stand by your side through the trials and triumphs, and to cherish our love, no matter what challenges we may face."

Thomas's voice, deep and steady, followed. "I, Thomas, take you, Martha, to be my wife, my confidant, and my partner in the pursuit of justice. I vow to protect and cherish you, to love you unconditionally, and to fight for a world where our love is not just tolerated but celebrated."

With their vows spoken, the pastor pronounced them husband and wife. They sealed their union with a kiss, their lips meeting passionately, their love defying the boundaries set by society.

As they pulled apart, Martha and Thomas were met with a round of applause and cheers from a small group of friends, family and supporters who had gathered to witness their special day. The couple beamed with happiness, their love shining brightly, a beacon of hope in a world still plagued by inequality.

The newlyweds spent their wedding night in a small inn, a safe haven provided by one of their friends. They dined by candlelight, sharing a meal prepared with love by the innkeeper. As they ate, they talked about their future, their dreams, and the challenges that lay ahead.

"We must continue to fight, Martha," Thomas said, his voice resolute. "Our marriage is a powerful statement, but it's just the beginning. We must use our voices and our influence to bring about real change."

Martha nodded, her green eyes shining with determination. "I agree, Thomas. We'll use our newspaper to spread our message even further. My parents will support us, and together, we can make a difference."

As the night deepened, they retired to their room, a cozy space with a four-poster bed draped in soft linens. Candles flickered, casting a warm glow over the room. Thomas helped Martha out of her dress, his hands gentle on her waist. As the fabric slipped away, revealing her hourglass figure, he couldn't help but marvel at her beauty.

Martha, in turn, unbuttoned Thomas's shirt, her fingers tracing the scars on his broad chest. She leaned in and kissed each scar, honoring the struggles he had endured. Thomas closed his eyes, relishing the sensation of her lips on his skin.

Their passion ignited, and they fell into a tangle of limbs on the bed, their kisses deepening. Martha's hands roamed over Thomas's muscular body, exploring every inch of him with a hunger that matched his own. He reciprocated, his fingers tracing the curves of her body, his lips trailing kisses down her neck, eliciting soft moans from her.

As their desire intensified, they undressed each other completely, their clothes discarded in a hurried frenzy. Martha's hands found Thomas's hardened length, and she stroked him gently, her touch sending shivers down his spine. Thomas groaned, his breath coming in ragged gasps as he reveled in her touch.

They moved together in perfect harmony, their bodies fitting together as if they were made for each other. Martha guided Thomas inside her, and they both gasped at the sensation. Slowly, they began to move, their rhythm building, their love making a powerful statement of their unity.

As their passion peaked, they cried out in unison, their voices echoing through the room. Afterward, they lay entwined, their hearts still racing, their love binding them together in a way that words could not describe.

The next morning, Martha and Thomas awoke to the sound of birds chirping outside their window. The sun streamed through the curtains, casting a warm glow over the room. They lay in bed, their bodies still intertwined, savoring the afterglow of their night together.

"Good morning, my love," Thomas whispered, his voice rough with sleep.

Martha smiled, her green eyes sparkling. "Good morning, husband. How does it feel to be a married man?"

Thomas chuckled, his deep laugh filling the room. "It feels right, Martha. It feels like the start of something extraordinary."

"It does. Are you worried about how the outside world will view our marriage? It is illegal."

"I know, I've been thinking about it. How would you feel about leaving the city. We can live in the countryside, in a rural area where there won't be anyone around. There we can share our love in the open."

"I'd like that. Of course o can still come to visit my parents?"

"Of course."

"Then it's settled, I can't wait to start my new life with you Thomas."

"As do I."

They kissed, their lips meeting tenderly, and Martha knew that their love was indeed extraordinary. As they prepared to face the unknown, Martha and Thomas knew that their journey had only just begun. Their love story was not just a tale of passion and romance but a powerful force for change in a world that desperately needed it.

Chapter 3

The warm glow of the campfire illuminated the serene woodland setting, providing a cozy haven for Martha and Thomas as they sought refuge from the turmoil of Philadelphia. The crackling flames danced, casting shadows upon their faces, reflecting the determination in their eyes. They had made a bold decision to leave the city, a place that had become increasingly hostile towards their interracial love. As they sat side by side, holding hands, the weight of their choice settled upon them, but it was a burden they were willing to bear together.

Martha, her fiery red hair cascading over her shoulders, looked into the dancing flames, her green eyes glistening with a mixture of emotions. She was leaving behind her parents, the comfort of her home, and the familiarity of the city she had always known. But the recent events had made it clear that their love was not welcomed by all. The attack by the angry mob, fueled by bigotry and hatred, had left an indelible mark on their hearts.

"I can't believe we had to leave like this," Martha said, her voice carrying a hint of sadness. "I never imagined I'd have to say goodbye to my parents so suddenly. It's not fair that we can't live our lives freely without fear of being attacked."

Thomas, his dark skin shimmering in the firelight, reached out and gently caressed her hand, his touch conveying the strength and comfort she desperately needed. "We'll make a new life for ourselves, my love. Your parents understand, and they want us to be safe. This land they've given us is a fresh start, a place where we can build a home away from the prejudice of the city."

Martha nodded, her resolve strengthening at the thought of their future together. "You're right. We'll create a sanctuary, a place where our love can flourish without fear. But I worry about the others, Thomas. There are so many African Americans still suffering in Philadelphia. I can't help but feel guilty for leaving them behind."

Thomas's eyes softened as he regarded the woman he loved. He knew the weight of her concerns, for he shared them. As a former slave, he had endured hardships and witnessed the cruelty inflicted upon his people. The scars on his back were a constant reminder of the injustices he had faced. But Martha's love had given him a new purpose, a reason to fight for a better future.

"I understand, my love," he said, his deep voice resonating with sincerity. "I, too, wish I could do more for our people. But we must also think of our own survival. We can't help anyone if we're not safe ourselves. This land, this new beginning, is an opportunity to build a stronger foundation. From there, we can find ways to support those who need it."

Martha leaned into him, seeking solace in his embrace. She inhaled the familiar scent of his skin, a mixture of earth and musk, and felt her worries begin to melt away. "You're right, as always. We'll make a difference, even if it's just for a few. And who knows, maybe one day we'll be able to return and fight for a better Philadelphia."

As they sat in silence, the warmth of the fire and each other's presence enveloping them, their thoughts turned to the passion that had brought them together. The bond between them was unbreakable, forged in the fires of adversity and strengthened by their shared ideals.

Thomas, his desire for Martha burning brighter than the flames before them, leaned in and whispered softly in her ear, his breath sending shivers down her spine. "I want you, here, now. I want to show you how much I love you, how much I cherish every moment we have together."

Martha's heart raced as his words ignited a fire within her. She had always admired his quiet strength and gentle nature, but when he looked at her with that fierce desire, she knew there was a wildness beneath his calm exterior.

"Make love to me, Thomas," she whispered back, her voice hoarse with longing. "Show me how much this new life means to you. Show me how much you want me."

With a swiftness that belied his size, Thomas stood, pulling Martha up with him. The firelight played upon their bodies, accentuating the contrast between their skin tones. Thomas's hands roamed over Martha's curves, his touch sending sparks of pleasure through her body. He lifted her dress, his fingers deftly unlacing the back, and let it fall to the ground, revealing her voluptuous figure.

Martha's breath quickened as she stood before him, naked except for her stockings and garters. The cool night air caressed her skin, causing her nipples to harden in anticipation. Thomas's eyes darkened with desire as he took in the sight of her, his hands itching to explore every inch of her body.

He reached for his trousers, unbuttoning them with trembling fingers. As he pushed them down, his manhood sprang free, erect and eager. Martha's eyes widened at the sight of him, her mouth watering at the thought of taking him inside her.

Thomas stepped forward, his hands cupping her breasts, his thumbs brushing over her sensitive nipples. Martha arched into his touch, her head falling back as a moan escaped her lips. He lowered his head, his lips finding her neck, and began to trail kisses down her body, leaving a trail of fire in his wake.

"You're so beautiful, Martha," he murmured against her skin. "So brave and passionate. I want to make you feel every ounce of my love."

His lips found her nipple, and he suckled gently, his tongue teasing the peak until she was writhing with pleasure. He switched to the other breast, lavishing it with equal attention, while his hands explored her waist, her hips, and the curve of her backside.

"Please, Thomas," she pleaded, her voice thick with desire. "I need you inside me. I need to feel you."

Thomas straightened, his eyes never leaving hers, and lifted her, wrapping her legs around his waist. He positioned himself at her entrance, the tip of his shaft teasing her wetness. With a slow, deliberate thrust, he entered her, filling her completely.

Martha gasped as he filled her, her body stretching to accommodate his size. She clung to him, her nails digging into his shoulders as he began to move within her, his hips thrusting in a steady rhythm. The fire crackled, the flames dancing in time with their passionate coupling.

Thomas's lips found hers, and they kissed deeply, their tongues entwining as their bodies moved in perfect harmony. He withdrew almost completely before plunging back into her, his strokes becoming more urgent as their desire escalated.

"Oh, Thomas," Martha cried out, her voice echoing through the woods. "I love you. I love how you make me feel."

Thomas's pace quickened, his breath coming in ragged gasps. "You're mine, Martha. Always and forever. I'll show you how much I love you every day."

Their bodies moved as one, their pleasure building to an intense crescendo. Martha's inner walls clenched around him, milking his shaft as he thrust deeper, harder, driving them both towards the brink.

With a final, powerful thrust, Thomas buried himself within her, his body shuddering as he spilled his seed deep inside her. Martha cried out his name, her orgasm rippling through her, wave after wave of pleasure washing over her.

They remained entwined, their hearts pounding in unison, as their breathing slowly returned to normal. Thomas lowered her gently to the ground, his arms never leaving her, and they lay on the blanket before the dying embers of the fire.

"I love you, Martha," Thomas whispered, his voice hoarse with emotion. "Together, we'll face whatever challenges come our way. Our love will see us through."

Martha smiled, her eyes glistening with unshed tears. "I love you too, Thomas. We'll build a life together, a life where our love can thrive. And who knows, maybe one day, we'll return to Philadelphia and make a difference for those who need it most."

As they lay in each other's arms, the night sky above them twinkling with stars, they knew that their love was a force to be reckoned with. The challenges ahead would be many, but together, they would face them head-on, fueled by their passion and unwavering commitment to each other.

Chapter 4

After a week hike outside of Philadelphia, Martha and Thomas found themselves in the small town of Green, Pennsylvania. The land that Martha's parents gave them was on the outskirts of the village. It was a blank canvas on which they could paint their future together.

Martha, her fiery red hair dancing in the gentle breeze, looked at Thomas with eyes full of determination and love. Her pale skin contrasted beautifully with his dark, rugged features, a testament to their forbidden love. She had always been a woman ahead of her time, unafraid to speak her mind and challenge societal norms. Her parents had raised her to fight for what she believed in, and that's exactly what she was doing now. Standing beside Thomas, she felt invincible.

Thomas Freeman, a man of remarkable strength and resilience, held Martha's hand tightly, his calloused fingers entwined with hers. He had endured unimaginable hardships as a slave, but now, standing on this land, he felt a sense of freedom and ownership. His muscular frame and the scars on his back bore witness to his past struggles, but his gentle nature and unwavering love for Martha softened his rugged exterior.

Together, they walked across the field, the tall grass tickling their legs as they went. The land was untouched, a perfect reflection of their untamed love. They imagined the home they would build here, a sanctuary where they could finally be themselves without fear of judgment or persecution. Martha's green eyes sparkled with excitement as she pointed towards the east, envisioning the sunrise flooding their bedroom with warm light.

"Our bedroom will have the most breathtaking view, Thomas. Can you see it? The sun rising over the horizon, filling our room with its warmth every morning." Martha's voice was filled with enthusiasm, her words painting a vivid picture in Thomas's mind.

Thomas smiled, his deep brown eyes reflecting the love and admiration he had for this extraordinary woman. "I can see it, my love. And every morning, I'll wake up to the sight of you, more beautiful than any sunrise." His voice, soft and gentle, carried a depth of emotion that only Martha could evoke.

They walked further, their footsteps leaving imprints in the soft earth. The land was theirs, and so was their future. They had faced adversity and hatred, but their love had only grown stronger. Philadelphia, a city on the brink of revolution, had become a hostile place for their interracial love, but here, in this field, they found solace and peace.

As they reached the center of the field, Martha turned to face Thomas, her body buzzing with anticipation. "This is it, Thomas. This is where we'll build our home. Our sanctuary. A place where we can love each other freely, without hiding." She placed her hands on his broad chest, feeling his heart pounding beneath her palms.

Thomas nodded, his eyes never leaving hers. "Yes, my love. This land will bear witness to our love, to our fight for a better future. Together, we will build a home, and a life, that others can only dream of." He pulled her closer, his strong arms wrapping around her waist.

Their lips met in a passionate kiss, fueled by the intensity of their emotions. Martha's lips were soft and warm, and Thomas savored the taste of her, the sweetness of their love. Their tongues danced, exploring each other with a hunger that mirrored their desire for a life together.

As their kiss deepened, Thomas's hands began to wander, caressing Martha's curves with reverence. He cupped her breasts, feeling the weight of them in his palms, and she moaned into his mouth, her hands gripping his shoulders tightly. The sensation of his touch sent shivers down her spine, igniting a fire within her that only he could quench.

Slowly, Thomas guided Martha down onto the soft grass, his body hovering over hers. The field around them seemed to fade away, leaving only the two lovers in their private paradise. Martha's heart raced as she felt the length of Thomas's erection pressing against her through their clothing. She wanted him, needed him, with an urgency that surprised even herself.

With skilled fingers, Thomas unlaced Martha's bodice, revealing her bountiful breasts. Her nipples, already taut with desire, peaked in the cool air, begging for his attention. He lowered his head, taking one rosy peak into his mouth, and suckled gently, causing Martha to arch her back and cry out in pleasure.

"Oh, Thomas... yes... please..." she panted, her hands threading through his hair, urging him on.

Thomas obliged, lavishing attention on her sensitive flesh, alternating between gentle suckling and teasing bites that had Martha squirming beneath him. His free hand roamed lower, tracing the curve of her waist before dipping beneath her skirt to find the heat between her thighs.

Martha's breath caught as she felt his fingers part her folds, already slick with her desire. He stroked her gently, his touch both tender and knowing. "You're so wet, my love. So ready for me," he whispered, his breath hot against her ear.

"Please, Thomas... I need you..." Martha pleaded, her voice hoarse with need.

Thomas kissed her deeply once more before rising to his knees. With deft fingers, he unlaced his breeches, freeing his erect cock, which stood proudly, eager to claim her.

Martha's eyes widened at the sight of him, her body throbbing with anticipation. She had seen him naked before, but the sight of his thick, dark shaft never failed to arouse her. She reached out, wrapping her hand around his length, feeling the pulsing warmth of him.

"You're so beautiful, Thomas. So powerful," she whispered, stroking him slowly, her thumb brushing over the sensitive head.

Thomas groaned; his eyes fluttering shut at her touch. "You make me feel that way, my love. I'm yours to command."

With that, Martha guided him to her entrance, positioning his tip at her slick opening. Thomas held himself steady, his breath coming in short gasps as he waited for her command.

"Take me, Thomas. Make me yours," she whispered, her eyes locked on his.

With a powerful thrust, Thomas claimed her, filling her completely in one smooth motion. Martha cried out, her body welcoming him, her inner walls gripping him tightly. He paused, giving her a moment to adjust to his size, before beginning a slow, steady rhythm.

Their bodies moved in perfect harmony, the grass beneath them rustling with each thrust. Martha's hands gripped his shoulders, her fingernails digging into his skin as pleasure coursed through her. Thomas's lips found her neck, peppering kisses along her sensitive skin as he drove into her again and again.

"Oh, Thomas... I'm so close..." Martha panted, her body tensing as the coils of pleasure tightened within her.

Thomas increased his pace, his own need for release building. "Come for me, my love. Let me feel you," he urged, his voice hoarse with desire.

Martha's climax hit her like a wave, crashing over her as she cried out his name. Her inner muscles clenched around him, milking his shaft as her body trembled in ecstasy. Thomas followed soon after, his own release spilling deep within her, his powerful body shaking with the force of his orgasm.

They lay entwined in the field, their hearts still racing, their bodies glistening with sweat. The sun continued its slow descent, casting a golden glow over the lovers as they basked in the afterglow of their passion.

"This land will be our haven, Martha. A place where our love can grow and flourish," Thomas said, his voice filled with conviction.

Martha smiled, her eyes sparkling with happiness. "Yes, my love. Together, we will build a home, and a life, that will be a testament to our love and the power of freedom."

As the sun set, casting long shadows across the field, Martha and Thomas knew that their future was bright, and that their love would be the foundation of the home they would build together. A home where their passion could burn freely, where their love would conquer all odds, and where their dreams would become reality.

Chapter 5

The sun was high in the sky, casting a warm glow over the small village of Green, Pennsylvania. Martha Wright, her red hair gleaming like fire in the sunlight, guided her plow through the fertile soil, preparing the earth for the upcoming planting season. She loved this time of year, when the land came alive, and the promise of a bountiful harvest was within reach. But today, her focus wavered as her eyes kept drifting towards the figure of Thomas Freeman, his dark skin glistening with sweat as he worked on their dream home.

Thomas, the man she loved, stood atop the roof of the log cabin they were building together. His muscular arms lifted and positioned heavy timber with ease, each movement showcasing his strength and determination. The sight of his powerful body, honed from years of hard labor, sent a rush of desire through Martha's veins. She admired his resilience, his ability to create a sanctuary for them with his bare hands, and the way he seemed to conquer every challenge with unwavering resolve.

As Martha plowed, her mind wandered, imagining Thomas's hands on her body instead of the plow's handles. She pictured him lifting her, just as he lifted those heavy logs, and carrying her to their bed, where they could lose themselves in each other. The thought of his touch, his kisses, and the feel of his skin against hers made her breath quicken and her cheeks flush.

Thomas, unaware of the effect he was having on his wife, paused to wipe the sweat from his brow. He took a moment to admire Martha's graceful movements in the field. Her pale skin, dotted with freckles, shone with a delicate sheen, and her red hair, loose and flowing in the breeze, was a sight that never failed to captivate him. He couldn't help but smile, knowing that this strong, beautiful woman was his partner in life, and together, they were building a future free from the constraints of society.

The day's work was exhausting, but both Martha and Thomas found solace in the physical labor. As the sun began its descent, they finished their respective tasks, feeling a sense of accomplishment and satisfaction.

They met at the edge of the field, their eyes locking in a silent understanding of the passion that simmered between them.

"You worked hard today, my love," Thomas said, his deep voice soft and gentle. "The field looks ready for planting."

Martha smiled, her green eyes sparkling with mischief. "As ready as I am for you," she replied, her voice laced with a playful tone.

Thomas's eyes widened at her boldness, and a slow grin spread across his face. "Then let's wash away the day's sweat and see what the night has in store for us."

Hand in hand, they made their way to the nearby stream, a secluded spot they had discovered during their first escape to the countryside. The water, cool and refreshing, beckoned them to immerse themselves in its cleansing embrace.

Martha, still in her white undergarment slip dress, stepped into the stream first, her feet sinking into the soft mud as the cool water enveloped her ankles. She let out a soft gasp, her body tingling as the water rose higher, caressing her calves and thighs. Slowly, she lowered herself, allowing the stream to envelop her completely, her red hair fanning out around her like a fiery halo.

Thomas followed suit, his tall frame making the water seem shallow in comparison. He was shirtless wearing only his trousers as he waded towards Martha, his eyes never leaving her as he moved with deliberate grace. When he reached her, he took her hand, pulling her closer until they were chest-deep in the stream, their bodies mere inches apart.

The water rippled around them, reflecting the fading light of the setting sun. Martha's pale skin contrasted beautifully against Thomas's dark complexion, their bodies forming a captivating tableau in the gentle current.

"You're so beautiful," Thomas whispered, his voice hoarse with desire. "I can't wait any longer."

Martha's heart raced as she felt his strong hands on her waist, pulling her closer. Their lips met in a hungry kiss, their mouths exploring each other with a fierce passion that had built up over the course of the day. Thomas's tongue danced with hers, their breath mingling in the cool air.

With their lips still locked, Thomas guided Martha towards the riverbank, where the ground was softer and more comfortable. He broke the kiss only to trail hot, open-mouthed kisses down her neck, eliciting soft moans from Martha's lips. His hands roamed over her body, cupping her full breasts and teasing her nipples to hardness through the thin fabric of her dress.

"Oh, Thomas," Martha breathed, her head falling back as she surrendered to the pleasure he was giving her. "I need you."

Thomas's hands moved to the laces of her dress, deftly undoing them, and the garment fell away, revealing her voluptuous curves. Her pale breasts, heavy and full, were topped with rosy nipples that begged for his attention. He lowered his head, taking one taut peak into his mouth and suckling gently, then with increasing fervor as Martha's breath grew ragged.

"Yes, yes!" she cried out, her fingers tangling in his dark, curly hair. "Suck them, Thomas. Make me come with your mouth."

Thomas obliged, lavishing attention on her sensitive flesh, his tongue and teeth teasing and pleasing in equal measure. Martha's hips bucked against him, her need growing with every touch. She wanted him inside her, filling her, completing the connection they shared.

"Please, Thomas," she begged, her voice hoarse. "I need you inside me. Now."

Thomas stood, his arousal evident as he shed his own trousers, revealing his muscular body and the scars that marked his past. He was a man who had endured much, but in this moment, he was all hers.

He positioned himself between her thighs, his hands gently spreading her legs wider. Martha's eyes locked with his, a silent plea in her gaze as she offered herself to him.

Thomas entered her slowly, his eyes never leaving hers as he filled her inch by inch. Martha's breath caught in her throat, her body stretching to accommodate his size. She was wet and ready, her inner walls clutching at him, drawing him deeper.

"You feel so good," Thomas groaned, his voice thick with desire. "So tight, so warm."

Martha arched her back, her hands gripping his shoulders as she urged him to move. "Yes, Thomas. Harder. Give it to me."

Thomas began to thrust, his movements slow and deliberate at first, but soon building to a feverish pace. Martha met his every stroke, her body rising to meet his, their skin slapping together in a rhythm that echoed through the quiet forest.

The sound of their lovemaking filled the air, mingling with the gentle rush of the stream and the distant calls of night birds. Martha's moans grew louder, her body trembling as she neared the peak of pleasure.

"I'm close," she whispered, her nails digging into his shoulders. "I love you, Thomas. I love you so much."

Thomas's eyes fluttered shut at her words, his own climax building. "I love you too, my sweet Martha. Always and forever."

With one final, powerful thrust, Thomas sent them both spiraling into ecstasy. Martha cried out, her body convulsing around him as waves of pleasure washed over her. Thomas held her tightly, his own release flooding her, their bodies becoming one in the most intimate of unions.

They lay entwined in the stream, their hearts still racing, their breath mingling in the cool night air. The water lapped at their bodies, a soothing balm after the intensity of their passion.

"I never want this to end," Martha whispered, her fingers tracing the scars on Thomas's back. "I want to build a life with you, here in this beautiful place, away from the world's judgments."

Thomas turned in her arms, his dark eyes filled with love and determination. "We will, my love. We'll build our home, raise a family, and live a life of freedom and love. Together, we can overcome any obstacle."

They kissed, a promise sealed with their lips, and then, with renewed energy, they made their way back to their land, their sanctuary in the wilderness. The night air was crisp, and the stars shone brightly, guiding them home.

As they lay together in their makeshift bed, their bodies still warm from the river, they spoke of their dreams for the future. They would finish building their cabin, plant their fields, and create a life together, far from the constraints of society. In each other's arms, they found the strength to face the challenges ahead, knowing that their love was a force that could overcome any obstacle.

The next day, as the sun rose over the mountains, Martha and Thomas awoke to the sound of birdsong and the gentle rustling of the wind through the trees. They smiled at each other, their love renewed and their passion burning bright. Together, they would build a life, brick by brick, love by love, in this wild and beautiful land.

Chapter 6

The crisp morning air of Green, Pennsylvania, filled the newly built cabin with a refreshing scent, marking the beginning of a new chapter in Martha and Thomas's lives. The one-bedroom log cabin, nestled amidst the breathtaking mountains, was a testament to Thomas's hard work and dedication. Every log carefully placed, each corner perfectly aligned, reflected his love for Martha and his newfound freedom.

Martha stood in the doorway, her green eyes sparkling with admiration as she took in the cozy interior. The small fireplace, crafted from local stones, added a touch of warmth to the room, and the kitchen, though modest, was a dream come true for the couple. She ran her fingers along the smooth wooden table, feeling the grain beneath her fingertips. "Thomas, it's perfect," she whispered, her voice filled with awe. "You've built us a home."

Thomas, his dark skin glistening with a thin layer of sweat from his labor, smiled proudly. His muscular frame filled the doorway as he joined her, his eyes searching hers. "I wanted to create a place where we could be truly free, where we can start our life together without the shadows of the past haunting us."

Martha's heart swelled with emotion. She knew the weight of Thomas's words. They had both endured hardships—she, as a woman speaking out against the chains of slavery, and he, as a former slave who had fought for his freedom. But here, in this secluded village, they had found solace and each other.

Without a word, Martha closed the distance between them, her red hair cascading over her shoulders as she wrapped her arms around Thomas's broad back. She felt the scars on his skin, reminders of his painful past, but they only made her love him more. "Thank you," she murmured against his neck, her breath warm on his skin. "I want to show you how grateful I am."

Thomas's eyes darkened with desire as he sensed her intention. He had always admired Martha's fiery spirit, and now, in this moment, he felt a burning need to possess her, to claim her as his own. He gently disentangled himself from her embrace, his hands cupping her cheeks. "You don't have to prove anything, my love. I know how much this means to you."

But Martha was determined. She placed a finger on his lips, silencing any further protests. "I want to, Thomas. I want to celebrate our new home and our love." Her eyes glinted with a mischievous sparkle, and she leaned in, her lips brushing against his.

Their kiss was slow and deliberate, a dance of passion and desire. Thomas's hands traveled down her body, tracing the curves of her hourglass figure, while Martha's fingers deftly unbuttoned his shirt, exposing his chiseled chest. The cool mountain air brushed against their heated skin, heightening their senses.

Guiding him towards the bed, Martha's movements were filled with a sensual grace. She pushed Thomas gently onto the soft furs that adorned their bed, his muscular body contrasting with the delicate surroundings. The afternoon sunlight filtered through the window, casting a warm glow on their entwined forms.

As Martha straddled Thomas, her red hair falling like a curtain around them, she paused, taking in the sight of her lover. His dark skin glistened with anticipation, and his eyes burned with a raw hunger. She reached down, gently grasping his thick shaft, stroking it with a firm touch. Thomas groaned, his hips arching off the bed, seeking more of her touch. "You're so beautiful," she whispered, her voice husky with desire. "I want to feel every inch of you inside me." With that, she positioned herself above him, guiding his length to her entrance. Slowly, she lowered herself, taking him in, inch by inch, her walls stretching to accommodate his size.

Thomas's hands gripped her hips, guiding her movements as she began to ride him. The bed creaked rhythmically with each thrust, the sound filling the cabin with their passion. Martha's breath came in gasps as she moved, her breasts swaying with each motion, her nipples hardening in the cool air.

"Fuck, Martha," Thomas grunted, his voice hoarse with need. "You feel so fucking good."

Martha's eyes fluttered shut as she savored the sensation of being filled by her lover. She quickened her pace, her hips moving in a wild rhythm, her juices flowing freely, coating his shaft with her essence. The scent of their desire filled the room, a heady aroma that only fueled their passion further.

Thomas's hands roamed her body, caressing her curves, squeezing her full breasts, and teasing her nipples until they peaked with arousal. He pinched and tugged at them, eliciting moans of pleasure from Martha's lips.

"Harder, Thomas," she panted, her voice laced with urgency. "Make me come."

Thomas obliged, his fingers working her clit with expert precision. He knew her body well, knew exactly how to touch her to drive her wild. As his fingers rubbed and circled her sensitive bud, Martha's hips bucked uncontrollably, her orgasm building rapidly.

"Oh, God!" she cried out, her body tensing as the climax washed over her. Wave after wave of pleasure rippled through her, causing her to grind down on Thomas's cock, her muscles milking him as she rode out her release.

Thomas, feeling her tighten around him, couldn't hold back any longer. With a final, powerful thrust, he emptied himself deep within her, his seed spilling into her welcoming warmth. He groaned, his body trembling as he surrendered to his own release.

They lay entangled in each other's arms, their hearts pounding in unison. The silence that followed was filled with the sound of their ragged breathing and the crackling of the fireplace, which had kept the chill at bay.

After a while, Martha raised herself on her elbows, her hair falling around her face in disarray. She gazed down at Thomas, her expression softening. "I love you, Thomas Freeman. I want to spend the rest of my life making you happy."

Thomas smiled, his eyes shining with love and contentment. "And I want to spend my life protecting you, Martha Wright. I'll never let anyone hurt you again."

A comfortable silence settled between them, but it was soon broken by Thomas's voice, his tone thoughtful. "You know, I've been thinking about my brothers and sisters still in chains. They'll never know the freedom we have here."

Martha's expression turned serious as she understood the weight of his words. "I know, Thomas. It's not right. But there are ways we can help."

Intrigued, Thomas propped himself up on one elbow, his dark eyes fixed on her. "How? We can't just march into the South and free them all."

Martha's face lit up with determination. "No, but we can help them escape. My parents have been involved in the abolitionist movement for years. They help organize safe passage for runaway slaves, providing them with food, shelter, and guidance."

Thomas's eyes widened as the implications of her words sank in. "You mean we could do the same here? Help slaves escape and find their way to freedom?"

"Exactly," Martha replied, her voice filled with conviction. "We can offer them a safe haven, a place to rest and recover before they continue their journey. With your strength and my family's connections, we can make a real difference."

Thomas's heart swelled with a sense of purpose. He had always wanted to fight for those who couldn't fight for themselves, and now he saw a way to do just that. "I'm in. We'll turn this cabin into a sanctuary, a beacon of hope for those who need it most."

Martha smiled, her eyes glistening with unshed tears. "Together, we can make a difference, Thomas. Our love will not only bring us happiness but also help change the lives of others."

As the sun began its descent beyond the mountains, casting a golden glow over the cabin, Martha and Thomas made love again, their passion fueled by a newfound sense of purpose. Their moans and cries of pleasure echoed through the cabin, mingling with the crackling of the fire, a testament to their enduring love and their commitment to the cause of freedom.

In the days that followed, Martha and Thomas worked tirelessly to transform their cabin into a haven for runaway slaves. They built secret compartments and hidden passages, ensuring that those who sought refuge would be safe from those who would seek to return them to bondage. The couple's love for each other only grew stronger as they worked side by side, their shared purpose forging an unbreakable bond.

But as they prepared to welcome their first guests, Martha and Thomas couldn't shake the feeling that their mission was about to become even more challenging and dangerous. They knew that helping slaves escape was not just an act of defiance but a declaration of war against the very institution that had kept them apart. Yet, they were ready to face whatever lay ahead, united in their love and their unwavering commitment to freedom.

Chapter 7

The sun had just begun its descent beyond the majestic mountains of Green, casting a warm glow over the quaint village. Martha Wright stood at the edge of the forest, her fiery red hair cascading down her back, a stark contrast to the lush greenery surrounding her. She breathed in the crisp mountain air, her green eyes scanning the peaceful landscape. The village, nestled in the heart of Pennsylvania, was a haven of tranquility, a world away from the turmoil of the ongoing revolution.

Martha's heart swelled with pride as she thought about her and Thomas's secret endeavor. They had found a way to make a real difference, to help those in need, and it brought them immense joy. The hidden compartments in their cabin, cleverly constructed by Thomas, had become a sanctuary for slaves seeking freedom. Word had spread quietly among the enslaved community, and each successful escape fueled Martha's determination to do more.

As the evening shadows lengthened, Thomas emerged from the cabin, his tall, muscular frame casting a long shadow. His dark skin, marked with the scars of his past life, glistened in the fading light. He smiled at Martha, his eyes reflecting the contentment they both felt. "Another day, another step towards freedom," he said, his deep voice carrying a hint of satisfaction.

Martha walked towards him, her steps purposeful. "We've helped so many already, but there are still more in need. I want to do everything we can to aid their escape." Her voice, filled with passion, echoed Thomas's sentiments.

Thomas nodded, his eyes softening at the sight of Martha's unwavering determination. "We will, my love. We'll keep doing this as long as there are slaves to be freed. I won't rest until every person is free to live the life they deserve." He reached out and took her hand in his, his rough fingers intertwining with hers.

Martha squeezed his hand, feeling the strength and warmth that always reassured her. "I know we can't change the world overnight, but we're making a difference, one person at a time. And I'm grateful we can do this together." She smiled, her eyes sparkling with love and admiration for the man who shared her ideals.

In the distance, the sound of approaching horses broke the evening calm. Martha's eyes narrowed, a sense of caution creeping in. "Someone's coming," she whispered, her voice laced with concern. "It might be another slave seeking refuge."

Thomas's body tensed, his instincts honed from years of hardship. "We'll find out soon enough. Let's get to the cabin; we don't want to draw attention to ourselves." He guided Martha swiftly through the tall grass, their feet silent on the soft earth.

As they reached the cabin, a man dismounted from his horse, his breath visible in the cooling air. He was a stranger, his face weathered and lined with worry. "I'm looking for Martha Wright and Thomas Freeman," he called out, his voice carrying a hint of desperation. "I was told they help people... people like me."

Martha stepped forward, her hand instinctively going to Thomas's arm. "I'm Martha, and this is Thomas. How can we help you?" She spoke with a calmness that belied her racing heart.

The man's eyes darted between them, as if assessing their sincerity. "My name is Jacob. I'm a runaway from a the plantation in Virginia. I heard about what you do here, and I... I want to be free." His voice cracked, and he lowered his head, ashamed to reveal his desire for freedom.

Thomas's voice, gentle yet commanding, filled the silence. "You've come to the right place, Jacob. We'll do everything we can to help you. Come inside, and we'll talk further." He gestured towards the cabin, his broad shoulders exuding a sense of protection.

Jacob hesitated for a moment, then nodded, his body language conveying a mixture of hope and fear. As they entered the cabin, the warm glow of the fireplace illuminated the room, casting shadows on the wooden walls. Martha offered Jacob a seat by the fire, and he sank into it, his eyes never leaving their faces.

"Tell us your story, Jacob," Martha urged, her voice gentle. "How did you hear about us?"

Jacob took a deep breath, his hands clasped tightly in his lap. "Word spreads among us, slave to slave. We hear whispers of people who help us escape. I knew I had to take the risk, to find you. I can't bear the thought of another day in chains." His voice broke, and he wiped away a tear with the back of his hand.

Thomas's eyes narrowed, his face a mask of controlled anger. "No one should have to endure such a life. We'll make sure you get your freedom, Jacob. We've helped many like you before."

Martha leaned forward, her eyes locking with Jacob's. "We'll hide you in one of our compartments until it's safe to move. Then, we'll guide you to the next safe house. From there, you'll make your way north, where you can live as a free man."

Jacob's eyes widened, and he shook his head in disbelief. "I can't believe there's a chance for me to be truly free. I thought this day would never come."

Thomas placed a reassuring hand on Jacob's shoulder. "It's a long and dangerous journey, but we'll do everything in our power to keep you safe. We've helped others make this journey, and we'll do the same for you."

As the night deepened, Martha and Thomas prepared a meal, sharing stories of their past endeavors, and Jacob listened, his eyes gleaming with newfound hope. The warmth of the fire and the camaraderie in the room eased Jacob's fears, and for the first time in years, he allowed himself to dream of a life beyond the chains of slavery.

After the meal, Martha showed Jacob to one of the hidden compartments, a small but well-ventilated space beneath the floorboards.

"You'll be safe here until we can arrange your next move. We'll bring you food and water, and keep you updated on our plans."

Jacob nodded, his eyes filled with gratitude. "I don't know how to thank you both. You're giving me a chance at a life I never thought possible."

Martha smiled, her heart touched by Jacob's words. "We're just doing what's right. We'll keep helping as many people as we can. That's our mission, and we won't stop until we've made a real difference."

As Jacob settled into his temporary sanctuary, Martha and Thomas retired to their room, the weight of their mission heavy on their minds. They knew the risks they were taking, but the joy of seeing people like Jacob find hope kept them going.

The following days were a blur of activity as Martha and Thomas coordinated Jacob's escape. They made contact with other abolitionists, arranging for Jacob's safe passage further north. Each day, they brought Jacob news of his impending freedom, his spirit lifting with every update.

On the night of Jacob's departure, Martha and Thomas accompanied him to the edge of the village, where a trusted guide awaited. Jacob's eyes shone with a mixture of excitement and trepidation as he prepared to embark on his journey.

"You've given me the greatest gift of all, freedom," Jacob said, his voice thick with emotion. "I'll never forget your kindness. I'll make sure to pay it forward and help others as you've helped me."

Martha embraced him, her heart full. "We're just doing our part, Jacob. Go and live the life you deserve. And remember, there are many more like us out there, fighting for the same cause."

Thomas clasped Jacob's hand firmly. "Stay strong, and keep moving forward. We'll continue our work here, and one day, we hope to see a world where no one is enslaved."

With a final nod, Jacob disappeared into the darkness, his figure blending into the night. Martha and Thomas stood there, hand in hand, watching until they could no longer see him. They knew the road ahead was fraught with danger, but they also knew that their efforts were making a difference.

As they returned to their cabin, the weight of their mission felt lighter, knowing they had helped another soul find freedom. Their love for each other and their shared purpose gave them the strength to continue, and they knew that as long as there were people in need, they would be there to help, one escape at a time.

The following weeks brought more slaves seeking refuge, and Martha and Thomas welcomed each one with open arms. Their cabin became a beacon of hope, a safe haven in a world filled with cruelty. As word spread, they encountered more challenges, but their determination never wavered.

One night, as they sat by the fireplace, discussing their plans, Martha turned to Thomas, her eyes shining with a newfound idea. "What if we expand our efforts? We could start a network, connecting with other abolitionists across the region. Together, we could help even more people escape."

Thomas's face lit up at the prospect. "That's a brilliant idea, Martha. We can't do this alone. By working with others, we can create a stronger, more organized resistance. It's time to take our fight to the next level."

And so, Martha and Thomas began to forge new alliances, reaching out to like-minded individuals and groups. They traveled to neighboring towns, sharing their vision and recruiting allies. Their love for each other only grew stronger as they worked side by side, fighting for a cause they both held dear.

As the months passed, their network expanded, and their success stories multiplied. Martha's fiery spirit and Thomas's unwavering strength inspired others to join their cause. They became known as the catalysts for change, a force to be reckoned with in the fight against slavery.

Chapter 8

The peaceful morning in Green, Pennsylvania, was abruptly shattered by the sound of galloping horses. Martha Wright, her fiery red hair cascading down her back, stood at the entrance of their sanctuary, her eyes narrowed with concern as she watched the approaching riders. Thomas Freeman, his dark skin glistening with the morning dew, stood beside her, his muscular frame tense and ready for any threat. The sanctuary, a haven for runaway slaves, was their pride and joy, a symbol of their unwavering love and commitment to freedom.

As the riders drew closer, Martha's sharp eyes recognized the telltale signs of British soldiers. Their red coats stood out against the lush green landscape like a warning sign. The couple had heard rumors of British loyalists searching for escaped slaves, but they had hoped their remote location would keep them safe. Little did they know, their sanctuary had become a target.

"Thomas, we have to act fast," Martha whispered, her voice steady despite the fear coursing through her veins. "Those are British soldiers, and they're heading straight for us."

Thomas nodded, his jaw clenched. "I'll gather the others. We'll hide the slaves in the secret tunnel and prepare to defend our home." His voice, though soft, carried an air of determination. He knew that their sanctuary was not just a place but a symbol of hope for those they sheltered.

As Thomas sprinted towards the main house, Martha's mind raced. She had never imagined their peaceful haven would become a battleground. The thought of violence on this serene land sickened her, but she knew they had no choice. Her parents had raised her to stand up for what was right, and she would not let fear silence her now.

The British soldiers, led by a ruthless officer named Captain Henry Bradford, arrived at the outskirts of the village. Their horses' hooves thundered across the green fields, sending birds scattering into the sky. Captain Bradford, a tall and imposing man with a scar across his cheek, surveyed the quaint village with disdain.

"Search every house, every barn," he ordered his men. "We have intelligence that this village is harboring runaway slaves. And if they dare to resist, show them the might of the British Empire!"

The soldiers dismounted and fanned out, their muskets at the ready. The citizens of Green, who had been going about their morning chores, were caught off guard. The peaceful Quakers, known for their non-violent ways, were now faced with a daunting choice—fight or surrender.

Martha and Thomas, along with a handful of brave villagers, gathered in the sanctuary's main hall. The slaves, terrified but determined, hid in the secret tunnel that led to the nearby forest. It was a well-crafted escape route, designed by Thomas himself, ensuring their charges had a chance at freedom.

"We must hold them off until our friends can escape," Thomas said, his voice calm but resolute. "I'll take the front, Martha. You and the others, defend the rear."

Martha nodded, her green eyes flashing with determination. She had seen Thomas fight before, and his strength and skill were unmatched. But today, they faced trained soldiers, and she knew it would be a fierce battle.

As the British soldiers approached the sanctuary, Thomas stepped forward, his large frame blocking the entrance. "You will not pass," he declared, his voice booming across the field. "This is a place of peace, and we will not allow you to harm those who seek refuge here."

Captain Bradford smirked, his eyes narrowing at the sight of an African man daring to challenge him. "You foolish rebel," he sneered. "Do you think you can stand against the might of the British army? Surrender now, or we will show you no mercy!"

Thomas's eyes hardened, and without another word, he charged. His powerful build and lightning-fast reflexes caught the soldiers by surprise. He swung his fists with precision, knocking one soldier after another to the ground. The villagers, inspired by Thomas's bravery, joined the fray, using farming tools as weapons.

Martha, at the rear of the sanctuary, organized a defense with the other women. They armed themselves with whatever they could find—pitchforks, shovels, and even kitchen knives. The women of Green were not accustomed to violence, but their determination to protect their homes and the sanctuary's cause fueled their courage.

The battle raged on, with the British soldiers gaining ground. Captain Bradford, witnessing the fierce resistance, ordered his men to set fire to the village. Flames erupted from the thatched roofs, sending plumes of smoke into the clear sky. The villagers fought with renewed vigor, desperate to save their homes and the sanctuary they cherished.

Just as the British soldiers were about to overpower the defenders, a thunderous roar echoed across the valley. A brigade of American soldiers, led by Colonel Benjamin Prescott, emerged from the forest. They had been tracking the British forces, hoping to intercept them before they reached the village.

"For freedom and justice!" Colonel Prescott cried, his voice carrying above the chaos. "We will not let these tyrants destroy what we hold dear!"

The American soldiers charged, their muskets firing in unison. The British, caught off guard by this unexpected reinforcement, began to falter. Captain Bradford, realizing the tide had turned, ordered a retreat.

Martha, Thomas, and the villagers cheered as the British soldiers fled, their defeat resounding across the valley. The American soldiers, though battle-weary, offered their assistance in rebuilding the damaged homes. The villagers, grateful for their help, welcomed them with open arms.

As the sun began to set, casting a golden glow over the charred remains of the village, Martha and Thomas stood amidst the wreckage, holding each other tightly. They had survived, but the cost was high. Many of their friends and neighbors had been injured, and the sanctuary had suffered significant damage.

"We must rebuild, Martha," Thomas said, his voice filled with determination. "We cannot let this setback deter us. Our love and our cause are stronger than any army."

Martha nodded, her eyes glistening with unshed tears. "We will, Thomas. And we'll make it even better. We'll show them that love and freedom are worth fighting for."

The villagers, inspired by Martha and Thomas's unwavering spirit, joined hands and formed a circle around the couple. Together, they vowed to rebuild their homes and the sanctuary, making it a symbol of resilience and hope.

In the days that followed, the village of Green transformed into a bustling hub of activity. The American soldiers, true to their word, assisted in the reconstruction, and the villagers worked tirelessly to restore their homes. Martha and Thomas, with their indomitable spirit, led the efforts, ensuring that the sanctuary would rise again, stronger and more welcoming than before.

As word spread of the village's triumph over the British, other runaway slaves found their way to Green. The sanctuary, now a beacon of hope, became a haven for those seeking freedom. Martha and Thomas's love, a force that transcended boundaries, inspired not only the villagers but also the wider region.

But the war was far from over, and the British loyalists were not easily deterred. Captain Bradford, humiliated by his defeat, vowed revenge. He gathered a larger force, determined to crush the rebellion in Green and make an example of the village.

Little did he know, Martha and Thomas, along with the villagers of Green, were ready for whatever challenges lay ahead. Their love, their sanctuary, and their newfound alliance with the American army would prove to be a formidable force, one that would shape the course of history in this small but significant corner of Pennsylvania.

As the sun set on another day, Martha and Thomas stood atop a hill overlooking the village, hand in hand. The air was crisp, and the scent of fresh pine filled their lungs. They had survived the battle, but they knew the war was not yet won. Their love, a beacon in the darkness, would continue to guide them as they fought for a future where all could live in freedom.

The story of Martha and Thomas, a tale of love, courage, and revolution, was just beginning. Their journey would take them through trials and triumphs, as they fought not only for their sanctuary but for the very soul of their nation. The British loyalists had underestimated the power of love and the resilience of the human spirit, and they would soon learn that the people of Green, Pennsylvania, were a force to be reckoned with.

Chapter 9

As the sun rose over Philadelphia, casting a warm glow on the bustling city, Martha Wright and Thomas Freeman prepared for a day that would forever change their lives. The young couple, united by love and a shared passion for freedom, had become symbols of hope and defiance in the eyes of many. Their story, one of courage and resilience, had spread like wildfire across the colonies, inspiring those who yearned for a better, more just world.

Martha, with her fiery red hair and determined gaze, woke with a sense of anticipation. She had dreamed of this moment, a chance to address the very government that held the power to shape their future. Her heart raced as she imagined standing before the state delegation, her voice carrying the weight of their collective struggle. She knew that their journey, fraught with danger and discrimination, had not been in vain. Their love had become a beacon, illuminating the path toward equality.

Thomas, his dark skin glistening with the morning dew, emerged from their modest lodgings, his muscular frame a testament to his strength and resilience. He had endured the horrors of slavery, but his spirit remained unbreakable. The scars on his back, reminders of a cruel past, only served to fuel his determination to fight for a future where such atrocities would be relegated to history. He smiled at Martha, his eyes conveying the depth of his love and gratitude for the woman who had stood by his side through it all.

The couple had arrived in Philadelphia a few days prior, seeking refuge and a platform to share their story. Word of their bravery had reached the ears of influential abolitionists and politicians, who saw in them a powerful symbol of the fight against slavery and racial inequality.

Philadelphia, a city teeming with revolutionary fervor, was the perfect stage for their message.

As they made their way through the crowded streets, Martha and Thomas couldn't help but notice the curious glances and whispers that followed them. In a city where racial tensions ran high, their interracial relationship was a bold statement, a challenge to the status quo. But they held their heads high, their love serving as an invisible shield against the judgmental stares.

They arrived at the grand statehouse, its imposing architecture a stark contrast to the humble cabin they had built together in the countryside. The building buzzed with activity as delegates from across the colonies gathered to discuss the pressing issues of the day. Martha and Thomas were escorted to a private chamber, where they would await their turn to address the assembly.

While they waited, Martha's mind raced with memories of their journey. She recalled the day they first met, when Thomas, saved her from that mob. There was something about his gentle spirit and unwavering determination had captivated her. From that moment on, their fates were intertwined.

They had fled together, seeking safety in the lush green forests of the countryside. There, they found solace in each other's arms and in the beauty of nature. They built a cabin, a haven for runaway slaves, where they shared their dreams of a world free from bondage. Thomas, a skilled hunter and cook, provided for them, while Martha, with her sharp wit and writing skills, documented their experiences, spreading awareness through her family's newspaper.

Now, as they sat in the heart of Philadelphia, Martha and Thomas knew that their story had the power to move mountains. They held hands, drawing strength from each other, as they prepared to face the delegation.

The chamber doors opened, and a hush fell over the assembly as Martha and Thomas entered. The room was filled with a diverse array of men, some in fine suits and others in more modest attire, all with the weight of their colonies' hopes and fears on their shoulders. Martha's eyes scanned the room, taking in the faces of those who held the power to shape their destiny.

The couple was invited to speak, and Martha stepped forward, her voice steady and clear. She recounted their story, beginning with the day they met and the bond that formed between them. She spoke of their shared vision, a world where love knew no color, and where freedom was a right for all. Her words were laced with passion and conviction, and as she spoke, the room seemed to hang on her every word.

"We have faced adversity, discrimination, and danger," Martha said, her voice trembling slightly. "But our love has given us the strength to persevere. We have built a sanctuary, a place where the oppressed can find refuge. We have fought for our right to be together, and in doing so, we have challenged the very laws that perpetuate injustice."

Thomas, standing tall beside her, added his voice to hers. "I was born into slavery, but I was blessed to find freedom. Freedom to love, to dream, and to fight for what is right. I stand here today, not just for myself, but for every man and woman who has known the chains of bondage. We are not asking for charity; we are demanding the rights that are rightfully ours."

The room was silent for a moment, as if the delegates were absorbing the weight of their words. Then, a murmur of agreement rippled through the assembly. One by one, the delegates rose to their feet, some with tears in their eyes, and applauded the young couple.

An elderly delegate, his voice shaking with emotion, spoke first. "Your story, young people, has touched our hearts and opened our eyes. It is a testament to the power of love and the resilience of the human spirit. We have gathered here to shape the future of our colonies, and your words have shown us the way forward."

Another delegate, a fiery-eyed man, added, "We have long debated the issue of slavery and racial equality. Your courage and love have reminded us of the urgency of our cause. We must act, not just for you, but for the countless others who suffer under the yoke of oppression."

The assembly erupted into a passionate discussion, with delegates from various towns sharing their own experiences and perspectives. The air crackled with energy as the room became a crucible of ideas and ideals.

As the debate continued, Martha and Thomas stood quietly, holding hands, their hearts filled with a mixture of hope and trepidation. They knew that their story had struck a chord, but they also understood the complexities of the political process.

Finally, after hours of passionate discourse, a resolution was put forth. The delegates proposed a bill that would not only abolish slavery in the colonies but also strike down the laws prohibiting interracial marriage. It was a bold move, one that would challenge the very foundations of their society.

The room fell silent once more as the delegates prepared to vote. Martha and Thomas held their breath, their eyes locked on each other, sharing a moment of unspoken understanding.

The voting began, and one by one, the delegates cast their ballots. The tension in the room was palpable as the votes were tallied. Finally, the result was announced. The bill to abolish slavery and allow interracial marriage had passed, and with it, a new era of freedom and equality was born.

The chamber erupted into cheers and applause, and Martha and Thomas found themselves at the center of a joyous celebration. Delegates embraced them, shaking their hands and offering words of gratitude and admiration.

As the initial euphoria subsided, Martha and Thomas were invited to share their thoughts on the historic decision. Martha, her voice trembling with emotion, spoke first. "Today, we have witnessed a triumph of love and justice. The chains of slavery and discrimination have been broken, and a new dawn awaits us. But our work is not yet done. We must continue to fight, to ensure that these freedoms are protected and extended to all."

Thomas, his voice steady and resolute, added, "This is a momentous day, but it is just the beginning. We must carry this spirit of unity and equality forward, into every corner of our land. We must educate, inspire, and empower those who have known only oppression. Together, we can build a future where love and freedom prevail."

The delegates, moved by their words, vowed to spread the message of freedom and equality far and wide. They promised to support the couple in their ongoing efforts to shelter and protect runaway slaves, and to continue the fight for a just society.

As Martha and Thomas left the statehouse, hand in hand, they were met with a throng of people who had gathered outside, having heard of the historic decision. Cheers and applause erupted, and the couple found themselves at the center of a spontaneous celebration.

The city of Philadelphia, a place once divided by racial tensions, was now united in joy and hope. The story of Martha and Thomas, two ordinary people with an extraordinary love, had become a catalyst for change, inspiring a revolution of the heart.

Chapter 10

As the sun dipped below the majestic mountains of Green, casting an amber glow over the peaceful village, Martha Wright and Thomas Freeman arrived at their humble abode, hand in hand. The long journey from Philadelphia had been arduous, but their love and determination fueled them every step of the way. Now, they were finally home, ready to begin a new chapter of their lives together, free from the shackles of discrimination and prejudice.

Their modest cottage, nestled amidst the verdant hills, welcomed them with its familiar warmth. The scent of pine filled the air, and the sound of the nearby creek provided a soothing melody. Martha inhaled deeply, feeling a sense of peace wash over her. She turned to Thomas, her emerald eyes sparkling with joy.

"We're home, my love," she whispered, her voice filled with emotion. "Our sanctuary awaits."

Thomas, his dark skin glistening with a fine sheen of sweat from the journey, smiled broadly, his eyes crinkling at the corners. "Yes, we are. And it's all thanks to you, my brave Martha. You fought for our freedom, and now we can build a life together, away from the hatred and bigotry of the city."

Martha's heart swelled with pride and love for this man who had endured so much. She knew the scars on his back, hidden beneath his shirt, were a constant reminder of the horrors he had faced as a slave. But now, in this moment, they were free to love and cherish each other without fear.

They stepped inside the cozy cottage, the wooden floorboards creaking beneath their feet. The interior was simple yet inviting, with a large fireplace dominating one wall, promising warmth during the cold mountain nights. A small kitchen area, equipped with a cast-iron stove, hinted at the delicious meals Thomas would prepare.

Martha's eyes lit up as she took in the familiar surroundings. "I can't wait to cook our first meal here. I've missed the fresh produce from our garden."

Thomas chuckled, his deep voice resonating through the room. "I'll gather some vegetables while you rest, my love. You must be exhausted after our journey."

Martha shook her head, her fiery red hair cascading over her shoulders. "No, I want to help. I've missed working alongside you in the garden. It's therapeutic, and I need it after all we've been through."

Understanding flashed in Thomas's eyes. He knew Martha's resilience and determination, and he admired her strength. "Very well, my dear. Let's tend to our garden together."

Hand in hand, they made their way outside, the late afternoon sun casting long shadows across the lush green grass. The garden, a vibrant patchwork of vegetables and herbs, welcomed them with its earthy aroma. Martha breathed in the familiar scents, feeling a sense of connection to the land.

They worked side by side, weeding and watering, their movements synchronized as if they had never been apart. Martha's pale skin glistened with a light sheen as she knelt in the soil, her hourglass figure accentuated by the simple cotton dress she wore. Thomas, his muscular frame moving with grace, kept a watchful eye on her, ensuring she didn't overexert herself.

As they worked, Martha's mind wandered to the events that had led them here. She thought back to the passionate speeches she had given in Philadelphia, rallying support for the abolitionist cause. Her words had inspired Thomas, and together, they had fought for their freedom, risking everything. Now, they were not only free but also expecting a child—a symbol of their love and the future they would build together.

"Thomas," Martha said, her voice soft and filled with emotion. She paused in her weeding, looking up at him with a mixture of love and apprehension. "There's something I need to tell you."

Thomas straightened, his dark eyes locking with hers. He could sense the importance of her words, and his heart quickened. "What is it, my love? You know you can tell me anything."

Martha took a deep breath, her chest rising and falling beneath her dress. "I'm pregnant, Thomas. We're going to have a baby."

Thomas stood frozen for a moment, his strong hands clutching the handle of the garden hoe. Then, slowly, a smile spread across his face, lighting up his entire being. He dropped the tool and took a step towards her, his eyes never leaving hers.

"A baby," he whispered, his voice croaked with emotion. "A child of our love. Oh, Martha, this is the best news I could have hoped for."

Martha's eyes welled up with happy tears as she rose to her feet, closing the distance between them. "I was so scared to tell you, but I knew you'd understand. I wanted to wait until we were safe here, away from the chaos of the city."

Thomas pulled her into a tight embrace, his arms wrapping around her like a shield of protection. He buried his face in her hair, inhaling the sweet scent of lavender that always clung to her. "You have nothing to fear, my love. I'm here for you, and I will protect you and our child with my life."

Martha's tears fell freely now, mingling with the sweat on Thomas's neck. She clung to him, feeling his heart beat against her own. "I know, my love. I know you will. But I can't help but worry about the challenges ahead. Being a mother is a daunting task, especially in these times."

Thomas gently tilted her chin up, his thumbs wiping away her tears. "We will face those challenges together, as we always have. Our love will guide us, and our child will grow up in a world we help create—a world free from the chains of slavery and prejudice."

Martha nodded, her resolve strengthening. "You're right, Thomas. Our love is a force to be reckoned with. And our child will be a symbol of that love, a beacon of hope for a better future."

Thomas's eyes darkened with a passionate intensity, and he leaned in, his lips brushing against hers. "Let us celebrate this news, my love. Let us make love, here in our garden, under the open sky."

Martha's heart raced at his suggestion, her body responding to his desire. She had always been captivated by his strength and gentleness, and now, with the knowledge of their growing family, her passion burned even brighter.

"Yes, Thomas," she whispered, her voice hoarse with need. "Make love to me. Show me how much you love me, and our child."

Thomas's hands roamed over her body, his touch sending shivers down her spine. He untied the laces of her dress, letting it fall to the ground, revealing her voluptuous curves. Martha's skin glowed in the fading light, her freckles forming a constellation across her shoulders.

Thomas knelt before her, his hands cupping her heavy breasts, his thumbs teasing her hardened nipples. Martha arched into his touch, her breath coming in short gasps. He lowered his head, his warm mouth closing around one taut peak, suckling gently.

"You're so beautiful, Martha," he murmured against her skin. "Your body is a wonder, a gift I cherish."

Martha moaned, her hands threading through his thick, dark hair. "Please, Thomas. I need you inside me. I need to feel your strength, your love."

Thomas stood, his powerful body towering over her. He swiftly shed his clothes, revealing his chiseled form, the scars on his back a testament to his past struggles. Martha's eyes drank in the sight of him, her desire growing with each passing moment.

He lifted her effortlessly, carrying her to the soft grass beneath a towering oak tree. The setting sun bathed them in a golden light, as if nature itself was blessing their union. Thomas lowered her gently, his body covering hers, their skin connecting in a symphony of sensation.

He positioned himself between her thighs, his hardness pressing against her core. Martha lifted her hips, seeking the fulfillment of their desire. Thomas entered her slowly, filling her with a pleasure that bordered on pain. She cried out, her voice echoing through the garden.

"Oh, Thomas! Yes, my love, take me. Make me yours completely."

Thomas began to move, his powerful thrusts sending waves of ecstasy through Martha's body. His muscles flexed and rippled as he drove into her, his eyes never leaving hers. Martha's hands gripped his shoulders, her nails digging into his skin, leaving marks of passion.

"You feel so good, my love," he grunted, his breath coming in short, sharp pants. "So tight, so wet. I can't get enough of you."

Martha's body responded to his every stroke, her inner walls clenching around him, drawing him deeper. She matched his rhythm, her hips rising to meet his, their bodies becoming one in a primal dance of love.

"Harder, Thomas," she pleaded, her voice hoarse with need. "Give it to me harder. I want to feel you deep inside me."

Thomas complied, his thrusts becoming more forceful, driving into her with abandon. Martha's cries filled the air, mingling with the sounds of nature—the chirping of birds, the rustling of leaves in the gentle breeze. Their bodies glistened with sweat, their skin slick with the evidence of their passion.

As their climax approached, Thomas leaned down, capturing Martha's lips in a fierce kiss. Their tongues danced, mirroring the rhythm of their bodies. Martha's legs wrapped around his waist, pulling him closer, urging him on.

"I love you, Martha," he growled against her mouth. "I love you so much."

"I love you too, Thomas," she whispered, her voice breaking. "Always and forever."

Their orgasms crashed over them in a tidal wave of pleasure. Martha's body convulsed around Thomas, milking his length, drawing every last drop of his essence. He roared her name, his body trembling as he spilled himself deep within her, marking her as his own.

They lay entangled in each other's arms, their hearts still racing, their breath mingling in the cool evening air. The sun had set, and the garden was bathed in the soft glow of twilight. Martha snuggled closer to Thomas, her head resting on his chest, listening to the steady beat of his heart.

"I love you, Thomas Freeman," she said, her voice filled with contentment. "I love you, and I love the life we're building together."

Thomas kissed the top of her head, his fingers tracing patterns on her bare back. "And I love you, Martha Wright. Together, we will create a family, a haven of love and freedom. Our child will grow up knowing only acceptance and compassion."

Martha smiled, her eyes closed, imagining the future they would share. "Yes, my love. Our child will be a symbol of hope, a reminder that love conquers all. And we will fight to ensure that their world is a better place, free from the chains of the past."

As the night deepened, they made their way back to the cottage, their bodies sated but their love burning brighter than ever. The fire in the hearth crackled, casting dancing shadows on the walls, as they prepared a simple meal, sharing stories of their journey and their dreams for the future.

In the quiet village of Green, Pennsylvania, Martha and Thomas had found their sanctuary. Their love, a force that had overcome adversity and changed history, would continue to grow and flourish, a beacon of light in a world still struggling to embrace equality and freedom.

And as they drifted off to sleep, wrapped in each other's arms, they dreamed of the day when their child would be born, a new life that would carry on their legacy of love and courage, and most importantly, this child will be free.

Don't miss out!

Visit the website below and you can sign up to receive emails whenever Michael Gordon publishes a new book. There's no charge and no obligation.

https://books2read.com/r/B-A-KEXRC-OLVIF

BOOKS 2 READ

Connecting independent readers to independent writers.

Did you love *Forbidden Freedom*? Then you should read *Will You Marry Me?*[1] by Michael Gordon!

[2]

The sun-kissed shores of Virginia Beach played host to a unique social experiment, a reality TV show that aimed to bring two strangers together in the hope of finding love. Among the eager participants were Zayden Moss, a charismatic former athlete, and Sabrina Chun, a reserved nurse with a rebellious streak. Their paths were about to collide in the most unexpected way, and the cameras were there to capture every moment. In the end of the experiment, will they stay married or be divorced? Find out in this season of Will you Marry Me?

1. https://books2read.com/u/4AlJdk
2. https://books2read.com/u/4AlJdk

Also by Michael Gordon

Will You Marry Me?
Love & War: The Battle of Virginia Beach
Forbidden Freedom

About the Author

Michael Gordon is a modern romance author who enjoys writing steamy, heart racing, interracial romances. When he's not writing, he's reading other swoon worthy interracial romance stories, traveling with his wife & kids, or watching sports.

www.ingramcontent.com/pod-product-compliance
Lightning Source LLC
LaVergne TN
LVHW091235150826
845673LV00003B/1140

* 9 7 9 8 2 3 0 5 1 7 6 0 3 *